YOU'RE THE HERO
PIRATE
ADVENTURE

Lily Murray

Illustrated by Stef Murphy

IVY KIDS

CREATE YOUR OWN PIRATE STORY!

D0526462

WELCOME HERO!

This book will help you create a pirate adventure story — and you're the main character! Here's how it works:

1
Read the question at the top of the page. You'll be asked to make a choice.

2
Look at the pictures and decide what you'd like to add to your story.

You're about to go on an adventure. Which one of these heroes do you want to be?

A warrior

A chimney sweep

A pirate queen

A toddler

A skeleton man

A knight

A skeleton woman

A goat

Remember — you're the hero! Add as many extra details as you want to shape your story. Tell it in your head, or read aloud as you go.

Once you're finished, go back to the start and see what happens when you make different choices. How many stories can you tell?

Or you can use this book however you want to tell a story. Your mission is to have as much fun as possible!

A parrot

A monkey pirate

A first mate

A princess

A grandpa pirate

A grandma pirate

A prince

A captain

Turn the page to pick some things to get dressed up in.

3
Read this part to get ready for the next bit of the adventure.

GOOD LUCK!
I'm coming too! Spot me hiding through the book.

You're about to go on an adventure. Which one of these heroes do you want to be?

A chimney sweep

A warrior

A pirate queen

A skeleton man

A toddler

A knight

A skeleton woman

A goat

A parrot

A monkey pirate

A first mate

A princess

A grandpa pirate

A grandma pirate

A prince

A captain

Turn the page to pick some things to get dressed up in.

What do you want to get dressed up in? Choose as many items as you like.

A pirate hat

A bandana

An eyepatch

Pirate boots

A beard

Lots of gold necklaces

Pink sunglasses

A rosette

An emerald ring

Gold earrings

Huge muscles

A belt

A crown

Hairy eyebrows

A pocket watch

Stylish moustaches

A rainbow scarf

Flip flops

A ruffled collar

A handbag

A bowtie

A striped necktie

A floral garland

A pair of gloves

Turn the page to decide where your adventure will take place.

Which one of these places are you going to visit on your adventure?

A desert island

Volcano-ville

Sweetie Land

The Antarctic

An underwater cavern filled with monsters

A cave full of hidden treasure

The Land of Knitting Grannies

A lush rainforest

A kingdom beneath the waves

A pirate milkshake bar

A forgotten city

The Island of Eyes

Caveman Cove

A country
ruled by pigs

Dragon Rock

A castle on a cliff

Turn the page to
pack for your
adventure.

Do you want to take anyone with you?
Choose as many crew members as you like.

A dog

A navigato[r]

A robot pirate

Nobody — you decide to go alone

18 of the best pirates you know

A bodyguard

A sea snail

Two dancing rats

A pet parrot

A cat

An experienced pirate

A flamingo

A ghost

A doctor

A cabin boy

A deck hand

Turn the page and decide how to travel in style.

How will you make your way to your destination? Choose one way to travel.

On a pirate ship

On a ghost ship

On a speedboat

In a bathtub

On a raft

On a bed boat

You'll ride on the back of a friendly shark

On a tanker

On a rowing boat

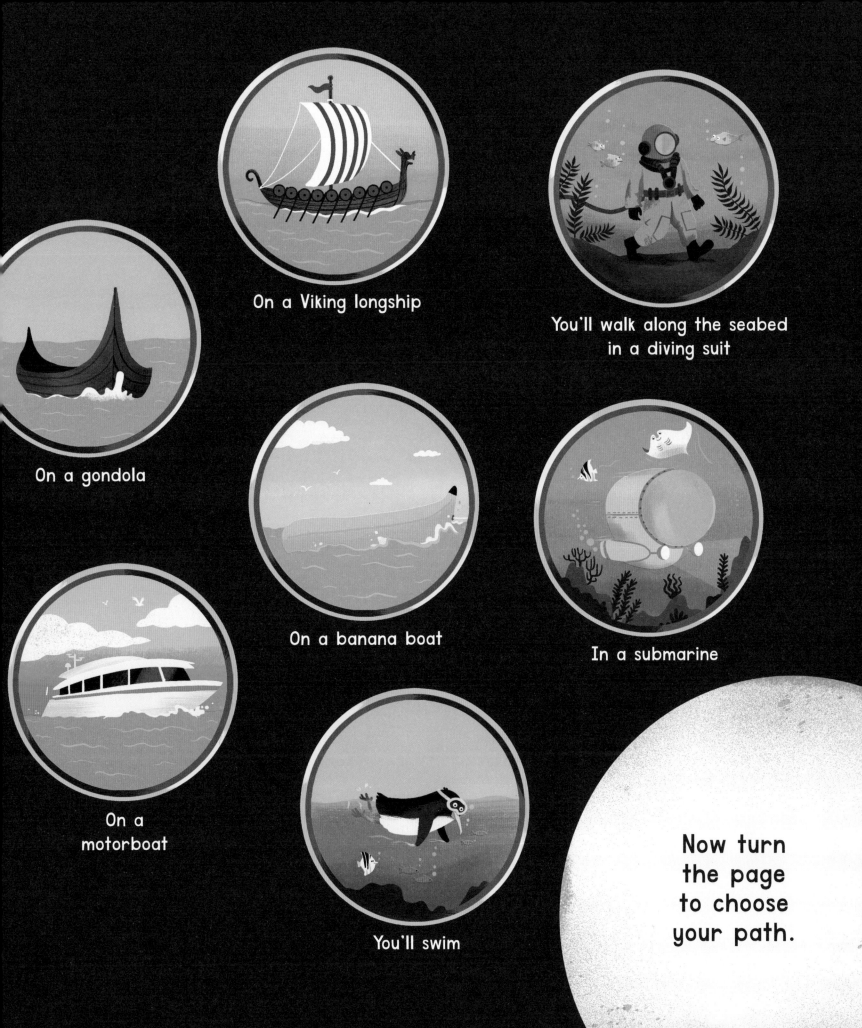

On a Viking longship

You'll walk along the seabed
in a diving suit

On a gondola

On a banana boat

In a submarine

On a
motorboat

You'll swim

Now turn
the page
to choose
your path.

Which one of these routes will you take?

Around ragged rocks

Through a storm

Past an island made of chocolate

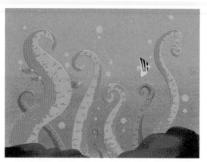

Through monstrous tentacles

Over the Sunny Sea

Into the Vampire Ocean

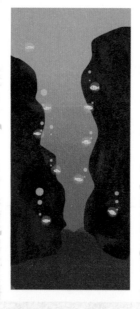

Past the underwater cliffs of doom

Down deep, past anglerfish

The northern route, through icy water

You'll follow a magic bird to your destination

The triangular route

Past Ballerina Bay

Over rainbow waters

Around Pizza Mountain

You'll circle a sea full of seals

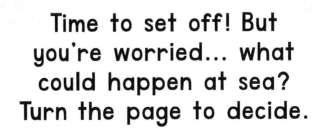

Time to set off! But you're worried... what could happen at sea? Turn the page to decide.

Zig-zagging around whirlpools

What are you afraid of during your sea voyage? Choose one terrible incident.

Meeting a hungry giant whale

Falling into the sea

Hitting rocks

Getting seasick

A cheeky seal stealing your hat

Rats eating all of your food

Being caught in a storm

A huge wave coming towards you

Being pulled into
the water by a
naughty mermaid

Getting lost
in fog

A sea monster
attacking you

Being forced to
walk the plank

Finding a
haunted chest

A cannonball
heading right
for you

Facing a
terrifying creature

Crocodiles
surrounding you

Phew – none of your fears come
true. You reach your destination
safely. Is someone waiting for
you? Turn the page to find out.

Yes, there's someone here
to greet you. Who is it?
Choose as many as you like.

Someone who
looks exactly
like you

A zombie
pirate

A llama

A band of
pirate musicians

An
iguana

A king
crab

A pearly
pirate

An invisible
friend

An alien

A mysterious pirate

A fisherman

A pug

A blue-bearded pirate

A diver

A gingerbread pirate

Pirate tots

They want to help you on your way. That's lucky, because danger is lurking around the corner... Turn the page to find out more.

An enemy has appeared! Choose the one you'll face.

A bad seal

A huge octopus

A monster alligator

An evil genius

A terrifying shark

Loathsome Captain Long-beard

A slimy jellyfish

A scary skeleton prince

Fearsome dino pirates

A big bully pirate

A hair-raising robot

Menacing Captain
Maggot-hair

Wicked pi-rats

A sly squirrel

Cunning Captain
Cutlass-beard

Reckless Captain
Red-hair

The enemy has an
awful thing in store
for you. Do you dare
to turn the page and
find out what it is?

What is the enemy going to do to you and your friends?

Set swooping parrots on you

Spring a shark with legs on you

Throw gunge at you

Force you to walk the plank

Point loaded cannons straight at you

Unleash their pet lizards on you

Hurl speeding barrels your way

Ambush you with their gang of thieves

Chain you to
a crow's nest

Tie you to
a ship's
wheel

Capture you in
a giant net

Feed you
to hungry
crocodiles

Attack you with a
cutlass-waving assassin

Release a trained
anteater to tickle
your toes

Toss you into a pit
of superglue

Open a trapdoor
beneath your feet

Have you met
your doom? Turn
the page to choose
how you and your
friends escape.

There's a way out! Which one will you choose?

You fight your way out using your sword skills

You do an enormous jump out of trouble

You're wearing invisibili socks! You activate them and run off

You boogie your way to freedom

You make friends with your enemy

You use your brain – you're a pirate genius

You suddenly become super strong and biff your enemy

Friendly dolphins race to your rescue

You spot a giant seabird and jump into its beak

You dive into the
sea and swim away

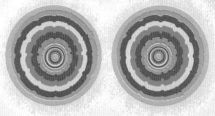

You hypnotize
your enemy

You transform
into a mermaid and
bewitch your enemy

You confuse your enemy
by wearing a fish
disguise, and escape

You craft
a rope from
seaweed and
swing away

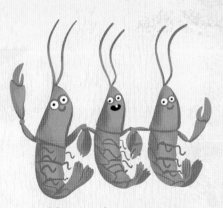

You get a group
of perky prawns to
pinch your enemy

You use treats
to make a deal
with your enemy

You all escape!
Turn the page
to pick a prize
for being such
a great pirate.

Which one of these things will you choose as your reward?

A lifetime supply of toilet roll

An exciting adventure is its own reward

The home of your dreams

Riches

Great friends

A sword

A pirate pal

A new treasure map

You become famous

A bigger boat

All the fries you can eat

A set of gold teeth

A magic lamp

An enormous trophy

A medal

A sparkly eyepatch

Your adventure is nearly over. There's just one more decision to make on the next page.

What happens next? Choose an ending for your tale.

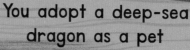
You sail off into
the sunset

You settle down and
run a shop

You become captain of a
different type of ship

You adopt a deep-sea
dragon as a pet

You go home and
get into bed

You hang up your
pirate hat...
forever!

You win a world record
for the longest beard

You take
a holiday

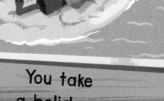
You start a
sailing school

You buy your own island

You join a pirate cheerleading squad

You become a famous pirate writer

You star in your own pirate TV show

You meet a pirate who tells you about hidden treasure. Will you help him find it?

You set up a rescue home for parrots

You have an enormous party to celebrate

You've told a brilliant story. Good luck on your future adventures!

First published in the UK in 2020 by

Ivy Kids

An imprint of The Quarto Group

The Old Brewery

6 Blundell Street

London N7 9BH

United Kingdom

www.QuartoKnows.com

Copyright © 2020 Quarto Publishing plc

All rights reserved. No part of this book may
be reproduced or transmitted in any form or by
any means, electronic or mechanical, including
photocopying, recording, or by any information
storage-and-retrieval system, without written
permission from the copyright holder.

British Library Cataloguing-in-Publication Data
A catalogue record for this book is available from the British Library.

ISBN: 978-1-78240-940-3

This book was conceived, designed & produced by

Ivy Kids

58 West Street, Brighton BN1 2RA, United Kingdom

PUBLISHER David Breuer

MANAGING EDITOR Susie Behar

COMMISSIONING EDITOR Lucy Menzies

ART DIRECTOR Hanri van Wyk

DESIGNER Kate Haynes

IN-HOUSE EDITOR Hannah Dove

EXTERNAL DESIGNER Suzie Harrison

Manufactured in Guangdong, China CC012020

1 3 5 7 9 10 8 6 4 2

THE END
Now go back to the start
and have another adventure!